Wish upon a Birthday

Wish upon a Birthday

By Norma Q. Hare

Drawings by Diane Dawson

GARRARD PUBLISHING COMPANY
CHAMPAIGN, ILLINOIS

For John, Dan, and Tom

Library of Congress Cataloging in Publication Data

Hare, Norma Q.
    Wish upon a birthday.

    SUMMARY: The first birthday cake ever is baked by a
poor cook's helper who cannot afford a present for the
princess.
    [1. Birthdays—Fiction. 2. Gifts—Fiction.
3. Bakers and bakeries—Fiction] I. Dawson, Diane.
II. Title.

PZ7.H2218Wi   [E]   79-14596
ISBN 0-8116-4418-9

Wish upon a Birthday

Gabe's cat, Stripes, purred softly
and rubbed her head
against the boy's leg.

He petted her gently
and gave her a bowl of milk.
"You'll have to stay
out of the way today,"
the boy told the cat.
"We will be busy getting ready
for Princess Melinda's birthday party.
The king has invited
everyone in the kingdom to come.
He has even asked all the servants."

Everyone in the palace was excited.
Princess Melinda could hardly wait
for her party to begin.

The servants talked of nothing else.
They had all bought fine birthday gifts
for the princess—
all, that is, but Gabe.

He was only a cook's helper
in the palace kitchen.
Gabe had a small room
and plenty of good food.
But he was not paid
for his work.

So he had no money
to buy a fine gift
for the princess.
Just then, the royal cook
rushed into the kitchen.
The door banged shut behind him.

"Ah, my boy!" he cried.
"We've a busy day ahead of us.
This will be a party to remember!
I've just bought
a beautiful red scarf
for Princess Melinda.
She'll think of me,
the royal cook,
whenever she wears it.
Have you bought
a gift for her yet?"
Gabe shook his head.
"I have no money
to buy a gift," said Gabe.
"But I may give the princess
my cat, Stripes.

She'd be a loving
and playful friend."
The royal cook
threw up his hands.
"Not Stripes!" he cried.
"Princess Melinda
is allergic to cats.

When she gets close to one,
her eyes get red, her nose runs,
and she sneezes giant sneezes!
No, you can't give her Stripes.

You'd better have a gift
by tonight,
or you'll be out
begging for food
and a place to sleep."
"I know, I know,"
Gabe said sadly.
He went to the flour bin
to get some flour.
The bin was almost empty.
"Run to the mill
and get us more flour,"
shouted the cook.
"We can't cook without flour.
And hurry, my boy!
There's no time to lose!"

Gabe pushed the cart
down the street
as fast as he could.
Stripes ran along beside him.
As they came to the mill,
Gabe saw the miller
running back and forth.
He was shouting
and waving his arms.
"Sir, what's wrong?"
asked Gabe.
"Mice! I'm chasing mice
out of my mill,"
shouted the miller.
"They're eating all the wheat!
Shoo! Away with you mice!"

Suddenly, he saw Stripes.

"There!" he shouted.

"Just what I need—

a cat to catch the mice."

"She's a good mouse catcher,"

Gabe replied.

The miller thought for a minute.

Then he said, "If you will let me

keep Stripes today, I'll pay you

ten pounds of my finest flour.

I'll bring her back tonight,

when I come to the party."

"All right," Gabe said,

"and thank you very much."

Then Gabe had an idea.

"Now I have a gift for the princess,"
he said happily.

"What is it?" the miller asked.

"I'll give her flour for her birthday,"
Gabe said.

"Flour?

What would she do with flour?"
asked the miller.

Gabe only smiled.

"We shall see," he said.

On his way back to the palace,

Gabe passed the egg man's house.

"Good morning, Gabe,"

said the egg man.

"What do you have in the cart?"

"I have a sack of flour
for the palace kitchen,
and some flour of my very own.
But I need some eggs.
Will you trade
some of your nice, fresh eggs
for part of my flour?"
Gabe asked.
"Yes," said the egg man.
"I was going to the mill for flour.
This will save me the trip."
"Thank you," said Gabe.
"Now I shall give the princess
some eggs for her birthday."
"Eggs?" laughed the egg man.
"What would she do with eggs?"

Gabe only smiled.

"We shall see," he said.

Gabe hurried on,

pushing the cart before him.

Soon he met the dairyman,

who was taking butter and milk

to the village market.

"Hello, Gabe," he said.

"What do you have in the cart?"

Gabe told the dairyman

about the flour and the eggs.

"I need some butter and milk, too,"

Gabe said.

"Will you trade

some nice fresh butter and milk

for some of my eggs?"

"Very well," said the dairyman.

"I can use some eggs."

"Thank you," said Gabe.

"Now I have some butter and milk

to give to the princess

for her birthday."

"Butter and milk?

What would the princess

do with butter and milk?"

asked the dairyman.

Gabe only smiled.

"We shall see," he said.

Gabe passed the candy shop

just as the candymaker

stepped outside for some air.

"Good morning, Gabe," he said.

"What are you carrying
in the cart today?"
the candymaker asked.
Gabe told him about the flour,
the eggs, the butter, and the milk.
Then he asked the candymaker
to trade some sugar
for some fresh butter and milk.
"All right," said the candymaker.
"I'll be happy to trade with you."
"Thank you," said Gabe.
"Now I can give the princess
some sugar for her birthday."
"Sugar? Did you say, 'sugar'?
What would the princess do with sugar?"
asked the candymaker.

Gabe only smiled.

"We shall see," he said.

At last

Gabe reached the palace kitchen.

All the servants

were helping the royal cook

to get ready for the party.

"Ah! There you are, my boy!"
the cook shouted.
"Bring in the flour.
My word!
What do you have in the cart?"

Gabe said,

"I left Stripes with the miller

to catch mice in the mill.

He was so pleased,

he gave me ten pounds

of his finest flour.

I traded part of the flour

for some eggs.

Then I traded some eggs

for butter and milk.

I traded some butter and milk

for some sugar.

Now I have a gift

for Princess Melinda."

"Upon my word,"

said the cook.

"What would the princess
do with flour and eggs
and those other things?"
Gabe only smiled.
"We shall see," he said.
At last
everything was ready
for the party.
The servants put on
their best party clothes.
The royal cook was very tired,
so he lay down on a cot
in a corner of the kitchen
for a short nap.
While he was snoring,
Gabe set to work.

After a while,
the cook awoke and sniffed the air.
"What's going on here?" he asked.
"Who is baking something?"
"I am," Gabe said.
"I've baked a gift
for the princess.
I've used my flour, eggs,
milk, butter, and sugar
to make her a big cake."

"A cake for a birthday gift?
I've never heard of such a thing.
Everyone will laugh
at a gift like that!" the cook said.
"Then they can laugh,"
Gabe replied.
"I've nothing to give her
but something I made,
and baking is what I can do."
"Well,
it's better than no gift at all,"
the cook said.
"My word!
Why didn't you wake me?
It's almost time for the party!"

He took off his apron
and smoothed his hair.
Then the royal cook
left for the Grand Ballroom
with the red scarf for the princess
carefully tucked under his arm.
Alone in the kitchen,
Gabe mixed a bowl
of soft, pink frosting.
He iced the big cake.
Then, all around the edge,
he put pink sugar roses
that he had made.
Suddenly
he saw it was very late.
He must hurry!

He lifted the big silver plate
that held the cake
and started to the Grand Ballroom.
But at that moment,
a gust of wind
blew through the palace halls.

It blew out
all the candles along the walls.
It was so dark
that Gabe couldn't see a thing.
He bumped into a wall
and almost dropped the cake.
He could never find his way
without some light.
Slowly
he went back to the kitchen.
A few coals
glowing in the fireplace
gave enough light
so he could find some candles.

Gabe stuck lighted candles
into the frosting
on top of the cake.
Now he could see
to walk in the dark hall.

Princess Melinda clapped her hands
when Gabe bowed low
and placed the cake before her.
"Happy birthday, Your Highness,"
Gabe said.

"What's this?" roared the king.
"Do you think
that is a birthday gift?
A CAKE?"

"Yes, Your Majesty.
This is the best gift
I could bring.
I couldn't buy a gift,
for I've no money.
This is a gift
made with my own hands."
Then the princess spoke.
"It's a beautiful gift, father.
I wish that everyone
in the kingdom
could have birthday cakes
like this one
on their birthdays,"
she said.
The guests smiled and agreed.

Gabe looked around
and saw his friends—
the candymaker, the dairyman,
and the egg man.
The miller was also there,
with Stripes beside him
in a small box.
"Well, well," said the king.
"Now it's my turn
to give my daughter a gift.
We've heard her wish
that everyone in the kingdom
could have birthday cakes
like this one on their birthdays.
I want to make my daughter happy,
but wishes shouldn't come too easily.

Therefore, I say,

if the Princess Melinda

can blow out

all the candles on this cake

with one puff,

I'll make her wish come true.

If not,

she won't get her wish."

Just then,

Stripes hopped out of her box

and walked over to the princess.

She rubbed herself gently

against Princess Melinda's skirt.

The princess' eyes grew red,

her nose began to run,

and her mouth flew open.

"Ah-ah-ah-CHOO!" she sneezed.
Everyone cheered,
for with that one giant sneeze,
all the candles
on the cake went out.

Her wish would come true.
Everyone in the kingdom
would have birthday cakes
just like hers.
The king turned to Gabe.
"My boy," he said,
"because Princess Melinda
is so happy with your gift,
you will become
the royal birthday cake maker.
From now on,
when anyone in this kingdom
has a birthday,
you are to make a cake
just like this one,
candles and all.

If they can blow out all the candles
with one puff,
perhaps their wishes
will also come true."
Gabe was proud
he'd made Princess Melinda happy.
He was also glad
he'd never have to worry
about birthday gifts again.
He would always
give birthday cakes for presents.
He felt Stripes rub against his leg.
"Thank you, Your Majesty," he said.
"But I couldn't have done it
without the help of my friends,
and Stripes most of all."